KU-147-890

TUMBLEWEED

He loves football but with only one leg it is very tricky.

He needs *HELP!!!*

Tumbleweed sighed, groaned and went ...

"YUCK!"

For Emma, Peter and Oliver who are the BEST .

g the "REAL" Tumbleweed

courageous little Bantam!!

Renew by phone or online
0845 0020 777
www.bristol.gov.uk/libraries
Bristol Libraries

PLEASE RETURN BOOK BY LAST DATE STAMPED

- 5 FEB 2011   1 6 NOV 2013
1 4 FEB 2011

2 8 FEB 2011   1 9 NOV 2014
1 1 MAR 2011

- 1 APR 2011

2 7 APR 2011

2 7 JUN 2011

2 2 JUL 2011

1 3 AUG 2011

2 7 AUG 2011
2 7 OCT 2011

BR100

BRISTOL CITY COUNCIL LIBRARY SERVICES
WITHDRAWN AND OFFERED FOR SALE
SOLD AS SEEN

d illustrated by Jacquie Hobbs Trajan

ght of Jacquie Hobbs Trajan 2009

1st Edition Print 2009

SG
21055 Print Services

IBSN 978-0-9562831-0-8

e moral right to be identified as the author / illustrator of the work. No part of the book may be reproduced or transmitted in any form or by any means, electronic or mechanical, including photocopying, recording or by any information storage system without prior permission in writing from the copyright owners and publishers. That it shall not without written consent of the publishers be lent, resold, hired out or otherwise disposed of by way of trade at any price in excess of the recommended maximum price or in mutilated condition, or in any unauthorised cover, or affixed to as part of any publication or advertising matter whatsoever. A CIP catalogue record for this title is available from the British Library.

Published by Barn-E-Bee Publishing
Bath. England
Please visit our web site : www.barnebeepublishing.co.uk
Printed in England

Bristol Libraries

1802467971

BRISTOL CITY LIBRARIES	
AN1802467971	
PE	12-Nov-2010
JF	£5.99

Twice in one day he had
been covered in muck.

The wind on the farm

was really quite **STRONG**.

And every time he blew

Tumbleweed just tumbled along.

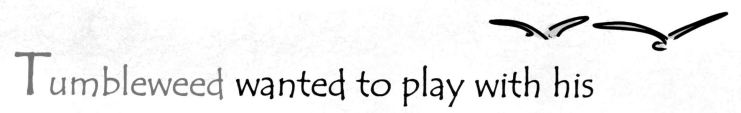

Tumbleweed wanted to play with his friends in the yard.

But having only one leg was making it **HARD**.

Then suddenly the wind blew once more.

Flying through the air was making him sore.

Then as he landed with a ...**BUMP**

in a feathery jumble.

A small voice called out "Wow what a tumble!"

"And the wind in the yard
just blows me around"

"He sneaks up behind me
not making a sound".

"Oh Tumbleweed " said Bert. "That will not do".

"But I have a **PLAN**...... that I know will help you".

So, with list under   wing Tumbleweed hopped away quick.

Collecting each thing ,,,,,,

.........first was a small stick.

Next, an acorn cup
from beneath the old oak tree.

A piece of old tyre was thing number **3**.

Tumbleweed took each thing back to the pixie's workshop.

Who worked very hard, Bert just did not stop.

From dawn until dusk, soon the work was all done.

Tumbleweed thought his
new leg was grand.

And when the wind blew
.....**YES**....he was able to
stand.

But what made Tumbleweed happiest of all.